A

DREAMER'S

HEART

A JOURNEY OF LOVE

THROUGH POETRY

BY

**CLAIRE DEAKIN
(DREAMWEAVER)**

EDITED BY: *LAVIN OWENDE*

JAYSONS ELIMU PUBLISHERS
P.O BOX 5121 – 80401 DIANI BEACH
EMAIL: jelimupublisher@gmail.com

MOBILE: **+254706392067/+254789954117**

Website: www.jaysonspublishers.co.ke

Distribution office: Ukunda town along Ukunda - Lungalunga Road, Kwale, Diani- Kenya

© **Claire Deakin**

ISBN: 978-9914-50-468-2

First published 2024
Published by Jaysons Elimu Publishers

Dreamweaver and Sam Ryder

DEDICATION

I dedicate this book to my Close Family and Friends.

Firstly to my friend Sam Ryder, as a thank you for all his inspiration and support.

Throughout the journey of our 'unique' friendship. During lock down I came across

Sam's music. The lyrics spoke to me and were very inspirational. I wrote a short poem entitled 'Dream Weaver' and tagged him on Facebook back in 2022. Not expecting anything until I received a direct message thanking me for the poem. We instantly connected and became friends. The journey of our friendship from what it was to what it is now has inspired so many of this collection. He encouraged me to follow my dreams and gave me belief in myself. Which is led me to finally get them published and become a published author. That first poem is where DreamWeaver was born.

Secondly to my husband, who over the 15 years that we have been together, I have written many a verse or poem for Valentines. Thank you for giving me your unwavering love and support. You are my rock and glue that has held me together.

Finally I'd like to dedicate it to my children Jordon, Robyn-Leigh, Jenna and Tilli. For all their love and support and encouragement. They all share my love and affection.

ACKNOWLEDGEMENT

Thank you to my close family, for all their love and support and encouragement. Times were tough and I almost gave up, but they encouraged me to write and share my poetry for others to enjoy.

I will forever eternally be grateful for Sam's inspiration and encouragement, from the beginning and whole entire incredible journey.

I would like to briefly thank my friend Ben Balogun, who assisted in adding artwork to my individual pieces before I shared them publicly.

Thanks also have to go to Mr Blair N Smith and Theophilus Agbu Clement, for coming across my poetry on social media. Thank you both for giving me the incredible opportunity to be part of a pioneering group of poetesses in The Poetess Book. For without their vision and dream, I would never have thought my dreams were capable.

And finally I would like to thank the Poetesses of that group. For sharing their own publishing journeys. Especially Lavin Owende (La-ki), for editing my work. I really appreciate her time and attention to detail and for letting me benefit from her experience, whilst helping me get this book out.

Thank you everyone much love and appreciation.

From DreamWeaver.

Note from Sam Ryder

Dear Claire Deakin,

I am writing this letter to express my deepest thanks for entrusting me with your moving collection of poems. Your words have formed intricate designs of feelings, thoughts and reflections that invite the readers into known and unknown realms.

The eloquence in your language and the profoundness of your mind cannot leave any living soul untouched. Each poem was significant in its own way and evoked a range of emotions that invited deep thinking. It is a story about poetry that shows how it can illuminate human existence, overcome barriers, and establish links across time and space. It is a compilation of beauty, sagacity, motivation that I feel so lucky to find myself among those who have pioneer these poem, and seen it written into existence. Thank you for sharing your gift with the world and for enriching my life through your words (Dream weaver Author). In anticipation I look forward to stepping deep into the realm of your work again; engaging through your poetic lenses more on the fabric called humanity.

With warm regards,

Sam Ryder

TABLE OF CONTENTS

PROLOGUE

Dream Weaver

Bring me all your dreams,

For I am your Dream Weaver

Bring me all your hearts

So, I can fill them with desire

Play the piano a sweet melody

So, we can all sing you me and everybody

Bring me a blanket, so I can wrap you love

For I am everywhere all of the above

Feel my hands holding onto you.

Always know I'm right beside you.

No need to pray at night for your dreams to
come true.

For I too are a dreamer I am yours, your Dream Weaver

X

It's All I Can Do.

It's all I can do, is try and stop myself smiling

Each and every time I think of you.

For nobody else has ever cherished me and my heart,

In the way you have done so from the very start.

It's all I can do, to stop myself from falling,

When deep down it is you my heart's calling.

When life and my heart beats erratic,

Thinking of you seems to do the trick.

It's all I can do, is to keep telling you

How much I love and care for you.

For falling in love is all I can do,

Each and everyday I fall more deeper for you.

CHAPTER 1

True Friend

To my dearest friend,

Who is truly a gift.

Your time that you share,

Shows me your love and care.

In good times and bad,

There are many more laughs to be had.

Through the hard times we will endure

For our bond is oh so pure.

True friendships last forever,

Through whatever we endeavor.

True friendships span the time,

I'm happy and comforted knowing you are mine.

Whether living far or near,
You will always have a friend my dear.
A friendship so close together,
There is no storm we cannot whether.

Old or new,
Near or far,
We will never be departed.
For my love for you,
Runs deep and true.
For this reason
I'll always be standing right next to you.

For Sam Ryder x

Treasures.

Just as there is Gold in the mountains,

And Pearls in the deep blue sea.

Neither of those treasures mean as much

As our friendship does to me.

Just to say I'm thinking of you,

Is something so simple but oh so true.

You're in my thoughts each and every day,

Even at night when I kneel to pray.

I'm always at the end of the phone,

For you my friend are never alone.

I will be by your side always,

For the remainder of my days.

I'll be there when you cry,

I'll be there when you sigh.

I'll be there when you're happy or sad,

For you my treasure are the best I've ever had.

Best Friends.

Best of friends can change a frown,

Into a smile from upside down.

The best of friends will understand,

Happy and sad go hand in hand.

The best of friends will always share,

Your secrets and dreams because they care.

The best of friends reach out and hold,

For they are worth more than their weight in gold.

A Budding Friendship.

How can you miss someone, you hardly know.

Missing someone is having them and letting go.

I could write a whole conversation all in rhyme,

About my love for someone that could never be mine.

I can take you on a journey of discovery,

To a land only for you and me.

Please don't blush, through my words

I don't beat about the bush.

My poetry is a way of putting my thoughts out there,

It's a way of telling people I care.

I can be there in any shape or form,

For my friendship goes beyond the norm.

If you like this poetry.

Then you will enjoy our friendship in all eternity

If I COULD TELL YOU

I could tell you, my dear,

The secrets held within my heart,

I'd whisper words of love and cheer,
And vow to never be apart.

If I could tell you, my love,

The dreams that dance within my mind,

I'd paint a world where stars above,

Would guide us, forever intertwined.

If I could tell you, my soul,

The depths of my unwavering trust,

I'd promise to make you whole,

In a bond that never turns to dust.

If I could tell you, my friend,

The gratitude that fills my days,

I'd thank you for being there till the end,

And for lighting up life's darkest ways.

If I could tell you, my sweet,

The melodies that sing in my soul,

I'd compose a symphony complete,

With harmonies that make us whole.

But words alone can't truly express,

The depth of what I long to say,

So let my actions, my love confess,

And hold you close, day by day.

Here I Am

And here I am

Sitting, staring at the stars

Amazed and bewildered

With the beauty of the moon

Admiring, it from afar.

Just like my love for you

I'm happy, watching and loving from afar

I know you are out there

Looking up

On the same moon and star.

And just like me

Wishing and hoping

One day our two hearts unite

Be together

Even just for a night.

Friends.

Whenever I talk to you my friend,

I relax and be myself for there is no reason to pretend.

We can chat for hours and hours

Because it is as important to me as this friendship of ours.

Our conversations will never run out,
We'll always find something to talk about.

Things become funnier while I'm with you,
For there is no time to feel blue.

My dear friend you will always be,
A special friend whose only there for me.

A rainbow or sun beam,
There is no in between.
For no matter what,
A friend in me you've got.

You are the person you are today
Because the people you knew,
Changed you in some sort of way.

Untitled

You toss and turn and wake up in a cool hard
sweat,

For I am the one you could never forget.

Nobody will ever know your fear

Of not being able to hold me near

Holding me year after year.

So, hold me close and don't let go

For I am a fan a friend who you already know.

One day

I will write to you but once a day

Until such a time you say go away.

Until such a time we get to meet

We can talk and rhyme until we greet.

Knowing all I have to say

Prevents you from walking away.

Your lyrics draw me close

Like a friendship I never want to lose.

I'm there for your highs and even more so
your lows

I know all your deepest secrets that no one
else knows.

I can bring you comfort, joy and even pain

So you feel like you're going insane,

I'll only stop when you call my name.

You

You are as high as a mountain and as deep as
the sea.

You are as wide as the ocean and as tall as a
tree.

You make me feel happy, when times are sad,

You are the bestest friend that I have ever
had.

You raise me up high,

When all I can do is cry,

You gave me a bed,

So I could rest my weary head.

I can never be sad when you're around

Because you lift me up clear off the ground

I feel like I can do anything with you by my
side

No more reasons to run away and hide

You make me sing make me shout

You told me to let it all out

For you my friend are a gem,

On you I can always depend Amen.

CHAPTER 2

Can't We Just Be Friends?

Can't we just be friends?

Possible but maybe more

Whatever the future intends

Never can quite be sure

Nothing is planned you'll see

Will only leave it to be guessed

Never know with me

But always up to a test

Still with that music playing

Come on get up on your feet

Don't bother in that seat to be staying

Some memories you have to stand to meet

Take me at my word

I know about this one

Living a story is better than one just heard

And you'll never know what's worth doing
until after it has been done.

Why?

Why now, when I'm not in a position to do anything?

Why do you make my heart skip a beat and flutter and sing?

Why are you so under my skin?

Why are you stirring sensations within?

Why are you so kind and make me feel appreciated?

Not at all how I anticipated.

Why after only a short amount of time?

Do I feel like I know you so well?

As if we were together in a previous lifetime?

Why does it feel so much like heaven? I'm glad it's not hell!

Why are you always on my mind?

Oh, how I wish you could be mine.

Why is our friendship so important to me?

Why are you probably the only person to actually get me?

I want to get to know you for the rest of eternity.

So, can you answer, why you're under my skin,

Or stirring sensations within?

Why is knowing you like being in heaven?

You by far stand out and are the best among all men.

I pray to God for that and say Amen.

Why are all these thoughts and feelings flowing through my head?

Is this what is preventing me from sleep while in bed.

Why can't I sleep and meet you in my dream?

Why is life so so mean?

I ask you and I, why oh why oh why?

Magic

Every day I believe in magic

And wish upon a shooting star.

For all the wisdom and logic

I can't touch you as you're too far

Here I am dancing and chancing with a
stranger

Not knowing or caring there could be a
danger

A lover's sigh lifts my spirits high

Like a shooting star across the sky

My longing dreams in all their eternity

Will surely come true eventually

Do you believe in magic that is inside you
and me?

A magic that's just bursting to be free

Lovers Sin.

It's just a laugh and a little flirt

Oh, what could that hurt

A little touch of the knee

If it doesn't bother you, it is fine with me

All for a little fun

Even when I am saying you're the one

Maybe you are

But let's not go too far

Now maybe I've been moaning

About some old sins I should be atoning

For those I'm not kidding

But that was when I was skidding

Only one more line to cross

Before all becomes a loss

You can get the entire

If for me you don't tire

You are.

You are a star,

I admire from afar.

You are the light in the sky

And the twinkle in my eye

You are the light autumn breeze,

Flowing gently through the trees.

Your journey started a long time ago,

Now you're out there for the whole world to know.

I hear your voice everywhere I go,

But seeing you is my ultimate dream you know.

I may be small in comparison to you,

Because after all, you are a star,

I admire from afar.

Do you believe?

Do you believe in shooting stars,

A flash of light in a cold dark night?

Do you believe a kiss in the rain,

Can wash away your pain?

Do you believe in adventures new,

Life as a child who used to be you?

Open your heart and soul and let her be free

Do you believe as the sun sets upon the
horizon?

Rainbows dance for no apparent reason

Do you believe in silence,

Where love is the only key?

Deep inside your heart,

Is where you'll find me.

We walk silently through the whispering
trees.

So, catch me quick before I go weak at the knees.

All along I wanted to know,

Do you believe in love at first sight?

I can tell by your face in the clear moonlight,

As it's illuminated.

I long for your touch,

The touch I've missed so much.

What are we?

Are we friends yet?
I can't really tell for sure!
I've been hanging around,
Recently trying to relate
And find some common ground!

I've been trying to clarify,
What it is between you and I?
Do we have common ground?

It's getting quite hard,

As I'm sure there's none to be found!

Are we acquaintances,

Friends or more?

I can't really tell for sure!

What do you say?

Are we growing closer or are we drifting away?

Is our bond being torn apart?

Are we to end up with a broken heart?

So, give it some thought,

at least for a day or two.

Then maybe you can say what

It is between me and you.

Are we acquaintances or friends?
Is there a label,
That can indicate if we are stable?
Can you relate to anything

And find some common ground?

So, I don't waste my time hanging around!

If we are more,

I want you to be sure?

If not then please tell me what is what!

I want us to grow closer, not drift apart.

I want us to be happy

And hold you deep within my heart.

I offer out a branch, an arm of friendship.

To be close, not joined at the hip.

But if you're not interested in
Anything like that,
Then please let me know so
I can turn away and go.

Forbidden Love.

Have you ever been in love with a person,

Strictly in a platonic way?

I'm trying to understand what you mean,

By the words you convey.

All that are heart felt but remain unspoken
between us.

Please feel free to talk,

Just so I can feel I'm not alone

By myself in this situation,

Having a single sided conversation.

That's sweet you call me by my name.

May it forever be always on the tip of your
tongue.

As you continue to luster and long,

Long for the connection to be made and to
become complete.

Happy knowing that you have solely swept me

clear off my feet.

The words flow through my mind onto paper,

For our conversations and our friendship are the inspiration I favor.

Call it fate, call it cosmic

I believe it's the universe working its magic.

Taking to you is like a comfy pair of shoes

You can sit and feel warm

And relaxed and never fear of being axed.

We can laugh and smile and chat for quite a while.

Walking hand in hand, barefoot across the sand.

For who could have known,

That I could have fallen

So completely and utterly in love with you.

My center a heart that beats with pace,

Left or right defines your grace.

Hedging my bets,

That you'll know where I am.

I'm your Dream Weaver author and your #1 fan

I'll be waiting for you to succeed in every way you can.

Talking to you is like a taking a gulp of fresh air.

Whisk me away,

I don't mind anywhere.

As long as I'm with you,

There is no place I'd rather be,

Than right beside you in everything you do.

New Years 2023

Sam as we are heading into the New Year,

Find comfort that there should be no fear.

You did a great job all throughout last year.

You went above and beyond.

For those for those unfortunate souls.

Who found themselves alone and, in the
cold,

With no food or shelter to call their own.

You do so much, much remains unknown.

May you continue doing so much good,

We had no doubt that you would.

May your music reach both far and near.

Spreading love and prosperous aloud and
cheer.

For you know the importance

Of putting your heart and soul in every
performance

You sing and dance

Whenever you have the chance

You gaze out across at scar

Whilst rocking it up playing your guitar

You flash us a smile

Every once in a while

Setting a date for your UK tour

Gets all your dreamers out of their doors

This one dreamer though wants so much
more

For Sam Ryder x

First Kiss.

From across the room,

In the light from the moon.

In the Opposite corner, someone locks their eyes

on you, soon enough your eyes meet

Your smile softens, you begin to blush

I slowly walk over to greet each other, steady there's no rush

I'm filled with a warm sensation,

I'm excited and full of anticipation.

An unseen force calls to my heart.

We are drawn in close, close enough to touch.

A deep sense of attraction pulls us together.

Emitting sparks of joy, as my body longs so much.

As I feel I've found you.
Silently I glance at the sky,
Silently my eyes and lips silently call to
you.
You stand amazed, as you take in the
view.
My stomach feels like a butterfly flapping its
wings,

Inside my heart sings. My heart sings a
song,

As you pull me in closer, with arms so
strong.

My heart doesn't rest,

Beating deep inside my chest.

The butterfly's wings have a gentle touch of
grace,

As are the petals of a flower, as beauty as
your face.

You both realise how the feelings feel
so strong
As hope becomes a colourful love song.
Invoking the sense of love.

Flying in on the wings of a Dove.

I realise how strong, and simple one small
touch can be,

As he slowly leans in and kisses me.

CHAPTER 3

I Choose.

I choose to love you in silence,

For in silence

I find no rejection.

I choose to love you

In loneliness,

For in loneliness

No one owns you but me.

I choose to adore you

From a distance,

For distance will

Shield me from pain.

I choose to kiss you in the wind,

For the wind is gentler than my lips.

I choose to hold you in my dreams,

For in my dreams you have no end.

Chat Poetry

(Me)

"I hold your hand"

I absolutely love, to hold your hand at night,

If I'm having a bad dream, it seems to make
it right.

When you toss and turn, your hand slips
away,

But then we reunite, and everything's okay.

(Him)

When you hold my hand, and whisper sweet
things.

Know that your loving touch, pulls at my
heart strings.

And when you're next to me, life is just
divine,

Walking into the sunset, with your hand in
mine.

(Me)

Taking walks with you,

Strolling hand in hand,

A simple show of love,

That we understand.

And when we stop our steps,

Your lips I do kiss,

I'll always hold your hand,

I promise you this.

A Locked Heart.

I put a lock on my heart before it got broke
Then I laughed out loud

Even though it wasn't a joke,

Figured I would play it safe

And step back from the flame

But I couldn't walk away

While it was calling my name

I floated like a moth

Attracted to a light

Going round and round in circles

In the middle of the night

I came in close

To get a better view

When I looked deep inside

It hit me out of the blue

There was a glimmer of hope

From what I could see

Might even give it another chance

If I could only find that key.

My Soul

As God watched over my failing body as I
sleep,

I prayed silently for my soul he gave to you
to keep.

You kept it well;

I can truly tell.

As you have never let my soul quiver,

As I have laid here full of aches and shiver.

It brings me piece of mind that you are
cherishing mine,

For your love for me is purely divine.

A moment of clarity from an aching head,

As I continue resting upon my bed.

Flourishing Soul.

From the moment I came across you,

And met you, you have stolen my heart.

And you are the only one with the key

To unlocking it and letting my flourishing

Soul out to fly free and tamed by one

... You

Your Voice

Over this past year,
I have listened to your voice in my ear.
Your songs went straight to my heart
As if shot from an arrow
I fell I love with you then
I love you today and tomorrow

There is no escape for me,
I'm well and truly under your spell.
I'm sure you know because you know me
well.
The ice in me melts
Leaving me with no doubts
I'm fond of you in every way
I have been since the very first day

HALO

Sam, you have a Halo of light,

That shines so bright.

It's like a beacon at sea,

On a dark winter night.

It shines both far and near,

Oh, how I wish you were by my side here.

The connection between you and I,

Is a love nobody can ever deny.

Loving you until the very end,

Is God's gift of a lifetime friend.

But you mean so much more,

Your sweet love is what dreams are for.

For Sam Ryder x

Forever

I wrote your name in the sky, but the wind
blew it away.

I wrote your name in the sand, but the
waves washed it away.

I wrote your name in my heart, and forever
it will stay.

All I Want Is To Love You Forever....

How can I explain about my love to you
when I have no barrier to feel your love?

How can I write about my love to you, when
I have no words for your love.

You taught me how to love you with my
heart and how to purify your love with my
soul.

My love for you is simple and deep with
affections and everyday flowing towards you
with happiness.

Loving you is something that comes easy from my heart and the reasons to love you more for your kindness.

Your love keeps me strong and brightens my soul every day and I cannot be myself without you being close to me.

You always hold me when I am down with tears and clutch me when I am down with pain. Now, All I want is to love you forever and is to grow old with you.

THANK YOU

Words aren't enough to express my upmost gratitude.

I sincerely appreciate your love and attitude.

The way you accept me, my faults and quirky personality.

Sometimes, I feel I'm not good enough, like I'm not worthy.

You believe in me, like no one else does.

It shows your confidence without any chaos

I thank you for being my inspiration

An understanding friend with no hesitation

I am with you forever to fulfil your every need.

I will hug you jubilantly rescinding my greed

I will solve your ambiguity and confusion

I will keep myself awakened to make you
alright with confirmation

Let my love last as long as the world exists

My hope never be shattered that I will resist

I love you for everything you are my heart
and soul

Your love is pure which will enable me to
reach my goal

If I could be

If I could be anything, I'd be the sun ☼

I'd shine brightly down on you

Making sure that you were OK wherever you were.

I'd be the breeze, rustling through your hair and the trees.

My gentle touch would remind you I'm always there,

Ready to embrace you and loyal with you in a playful way.

I'd be the thunder ⛈ storm to help cool you down and help you feel refreshed.

I'd be the stars and the moon, to keep you company at night.

But more importantly I'd be the reason your heart beats, and the song in your soul.

The twinkle in your eyes. I'd be everything and anything to you,

Because that is what you are to me.

A GIFT OF LOVE

She was more beautiful than nature,

Her soul radiated beyond compare;

But she was nothing without his vapour,
Nourishing the roots of her despair.

Without him, she was just a flower,

Withering away from her existence,

Needing him to give her a shower

So, her beauty could go the distance.

He knew without her, tides would change

And he would just be washed out to sea,
So he made sure to stay within her range
By holding onto her so gracefully.

The more he held on the greater they grew

And loves true beauty started to transcend

That was then, both their souls knew

They'd become more than just a friend.

Without each other, life wouldn't exist

As there would be no love to ever share

So, they embraced one another and kissed,
Showing just how much, they truly care.

Off Key.

As the moon pursues the golden sun

From you, I promise, I'll never run

You are the moon of my life forever

Faithfully I promise you this however

Off-key is the music of the night

Your heart to love is why I write

Lampposts burn away the pitch dark

To illuminate my love with their spark

I don't see your beautiful life off-key

I only see a perfect soul to set free

Born from deep pain and loss, I know

I see you like magic in the fallen snow

Rest your head, your weary eyes

I'll stay with you at lows and highs

I can love you until the stars expire

For you will never cease to inspire

So important this truth, my dear

I don't write it out of your fear

But rather to share with just you

The untold tale of my view

Since I've known you

Everything I think is channeled to you

A sense, a feeling, that can't be approached

I can't approach fate if it's already
approached by you

I can't refuse fate if I'm enchanted by you

I've been lost since I met you

You came to erase other destinies

Other ideas, other thoughts, other memories

And give colour to everything that the past
life erased

I've been lost since your arrival

Maybe damn, maybe bless, that left me
blind and deaf for life

Making me forget, everything I was and
what I am, enchantingly

Like an absolute surrender, announced in
your eyes

I look and see nothing since your arrival

I believe because I have to believe,

That love has gained a legitimate rhythm

I accept it now because I have no room for
doubt

About the charming and bright colour of
your eyes

And everything, I keep forgetting, like a
farewell

When I feel invaded inside

Now a thought, now a poem, now a dream,
now a passionate aroma

Of everything that conquers me inside,
definitely

I have no doubt that the mountain gave
birth to love

And this love child runs across the plains of
my heart

Among the verdant flowers of my passion

And the kingdom of solitude died in your
sweet presence, of this love

True love doesn't know how to die

When it's born, it's for real

Because it has the value of a life and a life of
love

And that's what I feel for you.

VALENTINE WORDS

Butter my bread

Sugar my tea

Be the first on my list

Be the last on my list

Come spend the time with me

I will always answer your questions

What we share in common is laws

I need you dear my valentine lover

I need you my only cover

Please be the blanket that will cover me

Be the bed I will sleep on

Be the pillow I will cuddle

Be my first

And also my last

The only person on my list

The only person my mind

Spend the rest of the day with me

Be the bee

So, you can produce your honey

My dearest Val

Be my ship

In this relation

Please do not capsize my heart

In the sea of lies

I will always be there for you

My dearest Val

My love

In the time of wave

These are my words this valentine for you

My first lover

My last lover and troubler.

What to say

What to say

If I already told you everything

Yesterday

Today

And tomorrow

I will tell you again

Will not be words

There will be kisses and hugs

Affection and love

Everything you will do

To understand

This love

What else

I will be able to say

Will make me feel

All I feel for you

Passionately each and every way.

True love

Be my heart, never let our love stray.

You are my rock, so I never drift away.

Kiss me please, but do it all the time.

You to me, are the perfect rhyme.

I'll never give you false hope.

We together will always cope.

Because our bond, has no boundaries.

Like hiding things in diaries.

We will never lie or deceive.

Our love is perfect, I believe.

You complete me in every possible way.

Loving you every night and day.

Me and you were always meant to be.

So, I write about you, in my love poetry.

TEACH ME TO BE PERFECT

I tried loving you then I'd hurt you

Deep in my mind wouldn't have done that to you

Am struggling to be good

Not to still spoil thy mood

You think that I'm rude

But you never understood

That I've got my own weakness

Am strong that am not fitness

I tried been your friend, I said to the end

I wouldn't pretend, I'll always amend

But sometimes I ware, still yet I do care

Sometimes my fear, had seem to appear

I want you to be happy you know that's true

I'll always be the one that'll still make it through

But sometimes I love you and sometimes it hurt

Sometimes deep inside am going through a lot

So that's why it looks like am always been wrong

I'm fighting my own demons can't tell for how long

I love you with my heart I wouldn't want you to cry

Am trying my best I can't tell you why

But my demons won't let me so they push me to the edge

And then at that moment am left with the pledge
A lot in my head, am crying in red.
Wish I was so perfect so perfect like the bird

But I wasn't born perfect that's all what we read

So if for me you'll accept,

Please teach me to be perfect.

Dreaming

Lay down your weary head,

Share my pillow upon my bed.

On the way to the fields of dreams, we'll take a detour.

I'll show you who my heart beats for…

Hold my hand and follow me,

We're heading towards the old oak tree…

Lay me down in fields of gold

And show me your 'bold'….

Cradle me in your arms,

Wrap me in your warmth.

Hold me close, smother me in kisses.

Your soft gentle touch is what my body misses……

I found you sleeping,

I thought it best to not disturb,

I stopped to watch you, you looked so
peaceful.

I crept on by happiness bestowed me,

Knowing that you would wake up refreshed
and rejuvenated

And not disheartened for not having met as
you had anticipated.

For even though you did not wake, you
knew I had come.

The smile on your face told me you were
having fun.

A Lover's Whisper.

Our ribbon hearts entangled

Together before we knew

'How long will it last'. I ask

'Forever' whispered you.

Kiss Me.

Kiss me quick, hold me tight,
never let me out of sight.
Kiss me quick, kiss me slow,

Hold out your hands and don't let go.

Kiss me here, kiss me there,

Kiss me just about anywhere.

Kiss me high, kiss me low,

Come sit beside me or you'll know

Just how much I love you so

Kiss me under the oak tree

Kiss me for all eternity

Hold me tight

Throughout the night

Let our love shine oh so bright

A Mortal Soul

I am all but a mortal soul, who wants to
share this moment like no other.

A love like mine can melt the heart,

A love so strong it will never be torn apart.

I long to hold my significant other,

But there are so many, I can't tell one from
the other.

When things go wrong, as they sometimes
will,

When every road you take, is always up hill.

When funds are low, and debts are high,

Always try to smile, instead of letting out a
sigh.

Keep pressing on and rest a while, when you
stop

For surely with perseverance, you will reach
the top.

For mortals like you and me,

Can be whatever we inspire to be.

Senses.

The sound of your voice as you call out my
name,

Reminds me that loving you is no game.

The touch of your skin,

Stir sensations within.

I open my heart for you,

For by now I'm falling in love with you.

The look in your eyes as you visually
undress me,

As in your mind's eye you play on fantasy.

The eyes are a window to our soul,

I assure you our love will never go cold.

The taste of your lips,

As I steal a kiss,

Is one I never want to miss.

The smell I crave,

Is that of your aftershave?

I like to be interment and help you shave.

For our love is oh so true,

I'd go to the end of the earth to be next to you.

Our love is like a kite, soaring way up in the sky,

Our love is so strong, nobody can deny.

Hold Me

Hold me close for the whole world to see.

Proves to me I am absolutely worthy.

Worthy of your time and love,

A love so pure like a dove.

A love so strong, it lasts a lifetime.

I'm happy knowing that you are mine.

Being together nothing can stop us

Or ever come between us.

Nothing at all in this whole universe,

Can ever stop me from being yours.

For as long as we have each other,

And you're holding me tight.

Our loving embrace, will last all through the
night.

DEEPER LOVE

When love comes from the soul

It's infinite, limitless seeking no parole

It's enduring

Always nurturing

Enriching the heart

With tenderness divine

It's there from the start

In all its subtlety sublime

Yet when its passion is unleashed

It creates such a yearning within

This is when a deeper love

Not only finds its way out

But also finds its way in

Enveloping you both

Just how love should.

CHAPTER 4

Friend or Foe.

Friend or foe,
I'm forcing myself to let go.

Things are not as they seem, who would
have thought that life could be so mean.

I fell for you, well the person I thought you
were.

For you being a lie, it did not concur.

I fell hard and deep,
All I can do now is lie down and weep.
A shell of my former self.

You had me fooled for a whole entire year,

For you knew exactly what to say
Exactly, what I wanted to hear.

The only good thing looking back
that I can take away from this,

Is my feelings and thoughts I put
into my poetry.

The feelings I am surely going to miss.

You were an intruder in my life and my
heart.

You came in and helped build it up only to
turn around and tare it into apart.

What to Expect.

The first time I laid eyes on you,

I thought I knew what to expect.

You held me around my neck,

As I placed my hand on your waist.

A smile filled your face,

I couldn't help but replicate lost in a
moment,

Found only in your embrace.

Our love blossomed like a rose,

Your familiar scent filled my nose.

Making it easy to breathe.

With you right by me,

If only we could see

Blinded by hesitation

We had too much expectations

I pushed you back,

When I felt the impact

Of my love for you,

Weighing heavy on my chest.

Thinking of what I said, by night I couldn't
rest

All I'm feeling is regret,

Can we rewind time yet?

It's been years since we spoke

And most nights my tears choke

Remembering what we had,

But still, I feel so glad

To have known you for your soul,

Even though I wish for more to make me
feel whole.

Every time I send a text,

You leave that shit unread

As you scrolled on by to the next.

If I saw you I'd tell you how I feel.

Everyday feeling this for real.

This hurt that controls my brain.

Do you feel a similar pain?

Like I'm missing a piece of me.

That I left with you.

I don't want anything new,
I just want the same old you.
I want things to go back to how they used to
be,
Just you and me for all eternity.

Heartache and Mistakes

Has our friendship ran its course,

We speak less and less.

My whole entire world is an utter mess.

If all was a game, then I feel the shame.

Over this past year I had grown quite fond
of you,

As you most certainly knew.

I couldn't imagine my life turning out any
other way

But now I think it's time to walk away.

There is too much mistrust and heartache,

To carry on would be a mistake.

Knock on my heart.

If you knock on my heart

You will hear the horror cries
And the echoes whispering of a woman
Who used to fly.

If you knock on my heart twice,

You will hear the story of a woman

Who used to love and trust

But now broken and unloved.

If you knock on my heart thrice,
You will find a crumbled soul.
But don't be upset

If you can't make it whole.

For many people left me

And the ones remained,
Tries to heal me.
But doubt etches in my eyes

For am a broken mirror glass

My happiness is tuned to silence

Where, I have gained badges of solitude

And on my chest, they are pinned

I'm almost gone

For this heart is like a grain

But I think,

There is something that can be done.

That is to make music once again

To knock once,

Then twice
And ten
times more
To hear the music of my heart.

A Wish.

If you were just a wish away

I'd call on every star

To bring you back from where you rest

To heal this broken heart.

If time were but a circumstance

Its whim not our demise

I'd stop the clocks to mark the time

I first looked in your eyes.

My wishes dim the starlit sky

'Till dark are all my hours,

In knowing I will never find

A finer love than ours.

Regret

I sang a song of tears for you,

It echoed from my aching spine

And whispered with the moonlit breeze

Oh, sweetest love, won't you be mine?

And should this sweet song reach your ears

Across the ageing, tired tide

I beg that you will take your heart

And hide it swiftly, deep inside.

For though I covet its caress

Upon my helpless, weary soul

I fear that I will turn it black

And leave you nursing but a hole

So, I will sing my song of tears

And mute the echo with my heart.

Where love, she blossomed once in vain

There now lay thorns and broken parts.

Hopeless Romance

I'm a fucking hopeless romantic,

Who wants love but can't it's so tragic.

I'm a tired hopeful person,

Who cries when I hear of love confessions.

I said I'm done of wanting and needing

But every time a glimpse of ghost swarming
in my mind

Mending of my broken heart is tearing me
blind

No one is true, not even you

So zip your thoughts, mind and all

For there's no one loves me flaws and all.

Sweet Dreams

You're either busy or asleep,

It's time for me to close my eyes

And begin counting sheep.

In my head I count 1 or 2

Before my mind wonders,

And I find myself thinking of you.

I pray to find that place of dreams,

Somewhere between the unreachable

And the unimaginable.

I'm sure with you as a guide somewhere in
outer space,

I should bump into a familiar face.

Someone to help ride those shooting stars,

That people wish upon.

The night doesn't last nowhere

Near long enough for me to go far,

Before I wake up from my slumber

To realise that you're gone.

Where did you go so suddenly,

You disappeared without a word goodbye.

I close my eyes and let out a sigh and
remember unfortunately you were never
there with me.

It was always just a dream.

A dream where nothing is as it should seem.

I close my eyes and see if I can find you
again,

Once I get close,

I shall start calling out your name.

So keep a listen out as you sleep,

I'm sure I'll find you laying there amongst
the sheep I'll be in your dreams,

Dancing in the moonlight.

Come find me if you dare and we can dance together all through the night.

Close and slowly, cheek to cheek,

Never having to speak.

Our bodies moving as one,

Under the moonlight my heart you have won.

She.

She thought she could ride the breeze

Over those old oak trees

And disappear from sight

But she didn't know it would be so hard

To navigate the shooting stars

Deep in the middle of the night

Because even as light as a feather

You can't stay up in the air forever

You're gonna float slowly down

So I have to wonder whether

She'll ever get it together

When her feet finally touch the ground.

She'll finally find love when she stops to
look around.

He Rides.

He either ride away

Or falls in love right from the start

He's always moving to the sound

Of thundering hooves or thundering hearts

He's riding those trails

Sleeping at night under the stars

Got a head full of dreams

An old soul covered in scars

He never stays too long

He wasn't made for the pasture

When he gazes at the horizon

His heart always beats faster

He longs for the prairie

And wide-open spaces

He'll slip out of the corral

Gonna leave behind the women

And all their beautiful faces

Without saying a word

Then ride like the wind

To stay in front of the herd.

If I Could

If I could turn back time,

To a point you weren't on my mind.

I could have said no,

While trying to turn and let go.

If I could be set free,

You wouldn't have such a hold on me.

If I could protect this heart of mine,

I wouldn't keep getting hurt all the time.

If I could rewind to the end,

I would have only have kept you as a friend.

I Never

I never meant to stumble into your life,

Or argue like a man and wife.

So, give me just a little time,

I'll head back over to my side of the line.

I never meant to bring strife to your life,

Or my words to cut you like a knife.

I'm sorry for all of this,

Our brief connection I will miss.

I'm sure that you will be alright,

Now you've came out of the darkness

And stepped into the light.

You have a bright future;

You don't need knowing me to be like
torture.

So it is with God's grace,

I pack up and leave your space.

Like I said I never meant to stumble into
your life

Or bring you strife.

I never meant to argue like a man and wife,

I never meant my words to cut like a knife.

Goodbye my short-term friend,

No more need to grin and pretend.

I'm Sorry.

I sorry my words and actions aren't enough,

For you see my life has turned very tough.

I'm sorry I can't help how you feel,

For what I'm going through is quite real.

Our lives are different, far beyond compare

Because each other's paths to cross we do not dare.

How can you or I, possibly understand what the other is going through?

When open and honest are no longer true

I'm sorry for how your coldness makes me feel

Your status makes it as no big deal

I'm sorry I am only small

I'm sorry you don't understand what I'm saying at all

I'm sorry that regardless of how much I plea

You will never truly appreciate the struggle I
see

I'm sorry our friendship isn't as all

Cracked up to what you thought it should
be.

I'm sorry I can't live up to your expectations,

I'm sorry you think I always have
hesitations.

I'm sorry for everything I have
said, I'm sorry for all I haven't
done.

I'm sorry you feel I'm the only
one, you feel you can turn to.

If taken the time you'll find that is untrue.

I'm sorry but when you eventually see,

There is no more friendship between you
and me.

I Shall Rise.

You ripped my heart out but that doesn't
matter

You were handed everything you ever
wanted on a silver platter.

You sat back and assessed the damage.

You made me look like a woman scorned on
a rampage.

No amount of gold could fill the cracks.

Our relationship had long time gone off the
tracks.

I thought you loved me;

I thought it was true I once was your
warrior,

I fought for you.

But I was forced to lay down my sword

And battle it out word for word.

But little did I know I'll rise from the ashes like a phoenix.

You better believe I will rise again and fix this.

But I will forever carry you by my side.

In my heart and soul. Together we shall ride.

For I was your wife and still in my heart play that critical role.

So even though your decision tore out my soul.

We will be forever bound together, not just in this life time but in all.

I was your queen, your equal. Standing next to you, standing tall.

Even though you left me a shell of a woman, I shall rise.

Right there In front of your very own eyes.

I love you still.

It drives me to insanity knowing I always will.

CHAPTER 5

Late at night in the river

I feel at peace
When I'm deep in a dream
Like an old oak leaf
I'm being carried downstream

Don't worry about the rapids
I know I'll make it through
Come out on the other side
Just a little black and blue

Guided by the stars
Pushed by the southern wind
I continue my journey
Up around another bend

There the water is calm
The world is completely still
And off in the distance
I hear my friend the whippoorwill
All my memories are waiting
They're calling out my name
Lined up on the riverbanks
Saying we're so glad you came
Those words touch my heart
It always makes me shiver
When I see them come to life
Late at night on the river

Sweet Music

Beautiful melodies sung in the morning
drown my soul.

Comforting rhythms clear my path when I'm
in deep sleep

Its sweet lyrics thrust my heart in the deep
pit I lie and   weep.

Thus, as its tune feed my ears,

Within its composure gives lessons.

I'll remember it through the years.

Music lights up my face

And its soundtracks quakes my body

Yes it can, but I only listen to one track

Good music soothes broken heart.

Especially when love is lost and you're torn apart.

It's lyrics mends punched hearts that were hurt.

Sing aloud jovially and let me be lost in it's waves.

My angelic voices echoes as if deep within the caves.

Love always

Don't be afraid

Love always

Be full of it

Love is a charm

Not a harmful substance

Do not use hypnosis

Just be in Love

And be the Love

It is not a sacrifice

It is a tasteful nectar

Love even when it is tough

Don't be tired

Don't let a broken heart stop you

Love and love some more

Love is not a snack

It is an ark to carry you across the river of living water

Into the everlasting Life

Love unconditionally

Love with your body, mind and soul

Love is a sacred garden

It is a covenant

Be in Love

Stay there

Don't allow logic

To govern your love life

Let it flow

Love is a fluid

Fill it into every heart

And watch as life is nourished

Be the light that opens the gates of eternity

Love is the key to the secret of life

Hold it in you

And the doors of everything will open

Nothingness will be your fulfilment

Happiness will follow you

Peace will be with you

Love is not a seductive substance

It is a sacred place with no end

A beautiful existence beyond logic

Love and always be in Love

Nothing but beauty and magic.

My Dreams

Life throws things at me

Sometimes it's a ping pong ball

Floating in and out of consciousness

The game is not real, but the dream is a big
deal

Sometimes I am a flower inside the heart of
my man

And my petals are black and white

All the colours drained

Like a desert longing for rain

I long for the colourful life

The feelings of attachment,
identities and achievements
permeate my thoughts
But the dream keeps me away from that
reality

Into the dimensionless realm of nothingness

Here I am a nest awaiting the arrival of my
tenants

I have neither knowledge nor understanding

Just a template of life

In my dream, I am a tabernacle of being

Far away from this physical world

Yet present inside every one of you

Locked away inside the mystery

Hidden from sight

Alone in the aloneness

I yearn for all of you
to be here with me

But it's close to
impossible for you to
hear me

It's my prayer, to be with you

To get to know you

To embrace your world

But the veil of mystery separates us for now

I wonder if the time will come for me to
wake up

And be with you

Or for you to finally answer my prayer

And come inside the substance of being

It is my dream for you to know your true
self

If You Fall In Love.

If you fall in love, because someone makes
you laugh.

Hold onto them a little longer.

Sometimes though the time you have,

is never quite enough.

What happens when you no longer find
them funny.

Someone else may never get your hunny.

If you fall in love, because someone is
beautiful.

Make sure there is more to them.

Otherwise, you'll be wondering

What will happen when their out beauty
fades.

That's why inner beauty is the best,

It should hold its own against any test.

If you fall in love, because someone can
provide for you.

What would happen when they're no longer
able to?

What happens if they lose all their wealth,

Due to poor decisions or I'll health?

Real love defies all odds and all reasons.

It lasts throughout all seasons.

When you truly love someone, you do not
look for reasons.

You look through their soul and see beyond
them.

For only then when true love has finally
came,

Only then will you receive a love so pure
time and time again.

Well Wishes.

I hope your OK, sleeping well and getting
plenty of rest.

So, you can continue doing your best.

Time after time,

You may fall out of line.

But you always bounce back,

You have a knack of getting back on track.

Go follow your dream,

Moving forward, not looking where you have
been.

No time for feeling blue,

Not when you have your whole future ahead
of you.

Go and showcase the best of you.

Is all that I want you to do.

Step aside and reach up far,

Like the shining star that you are.

Go shine your light so bright,

Go shine on all through the night.

You are the most vibrant star in sight.

Take comfort in knowing and try not despair,

I may be in body here but I'm always in spirit there.

Dance in The Rain

Don't wait for the storm to pass, learn to dance in the rain.

Those sweet falling raindrops, will never put out your flame

Spinning around in circles, with your face to the sky

Is one of life's simple pleasures, that no money can buy

If the night is a mystery, don't wait for the sun to rise

You can still find your way, with the moonlight in your eyes

A warm southern breeze, gently guiding you along

A woodpecker keeping rhythm, knocking out a song

After a bolt of lightning, you're gonna feel
the thunder

Instead of being afraid, take a minute and
wonder

What does it
mean, when it
comes down from
above How does
it feel, to be
floating on the
wings of love.

It's a night to remember, with static in the
air

The world at a distance and wind in your
hair

You'll always taste the sweetness, of the rain
on your tongue
Long after you've forgotten, what it means to
be young

My Words.

There is not much to say,

Apart from my words can paint a picture in my mind.

My work depends on my mood.

As I have said so many times before,

Nothing or anyone in particular inspires me.

My words just flow with ease through me.

No pretense, these are my words as they tumble through my mind.

Until pen to paper do I find.

I am happy standing in the shadows of my words.

Instead of trying to shine because my inner light,

Is not so bright.

I let my words tell you, my story.

As I don't like to let people see the real me.

My words can reach further than I can ever
expect to travel. Far beyond the land and
sky, or any distance between you and I.

My words can make you happy,

Whenever you're feeling down. They can
guide you through the darkness when the
sun goes down.

Like the moon,

They can guide the way.

As you continue on your way.

My words are kind and sincere and true.

I can use them to tell you every little thing
about you.

I won't sugar coat,

Or insist we're in the same boat.

You can choose to listen or ignore;

I'll tell you again like I have once before.

I choose to remain in the shadows,

To tell my story that nobody knows.

I would lend you a candle,

For a light you can handle.

As like I said my inner light doesn't shine so bright.

Use the candle and stay close to me to hear all my words that I have to say.

About all the things I've seen along the way.

My words can take you on a journey of twists and turns, highs and lows.

Through a land of wonder nobody else knows.

I can use them to paint a picture so you can see,

All the beautiful things that are surrounding
me.

From the birds in the trees to the animals
on the ground. There is so much to see, if
you stop and look around.

There is truly beauty in this vast land.

Come with me and I'll show you around.

The animals and places, there is so much to
see.

I can never get bored of using my words to
help you see visually.

The time has come for me to come out from
the shadows.

So people can put a face to the author of
words that they know.

My inner light is shining brighter,

as my journey continues through the night
into the day where it is lighter.

You can see for yourself, all that I have told you about. From the birds in the trees to the animals on the ground.

You can see the true beauty of this vast land.

No more need to guide you or show you around.

I'll still use my words each and every day, because they bring happiness and sunshine with every word I say.

About Me.

"About Me? About You?"

Songs I write and poems I pen,

And all the stories,

they contain within,

Are they true to my life? Do you want to know?

Well, they're probably not but maybe so.

My words are inspired by world events, just old stories, all past tense.

Songs about life, in a familiar key,

But it doesn't mean they're all about me.

My writings may include, family and friends,

Or relationships coming to bitter ends.

Silly things that some people do,

Hell, my poems could even be about you.

So, I'll bring this story to a gentle close,

Who I write about, no one knows.

I never really know how a poem may go,

But when I figure them out, I'll let you know.

Twilight

A time between day and night,

A magical moment, of golden light.

The sky transforms, with hues so bright,

Paintbrush of colours, a true delight.

As the sun sets, the day bids adieu,

The world transforms, in a hue of blue.

The birds return, to their nest and sing,

A lullaby of peace, on the horizon they bring.

The stars twinkle, like diamonds in the sky,

A celestial symphony, that never says goodbye.

The moon rises, with its soft silvery shine,

Guiding us gently, through the night that's so divine.

Twilight is a time, of stillness and calm,

A time to reflect, on life's journey so warm.

A time to let go, of worries and strife,

And bask in the beauty, of this peaceful life.

So let's cherish this moment, of quiet and
peace,

And enjoy the magic, of this gorgeous
release.

For twilight is fleeting, and gone all too
soon,

But its memory lingers, in the light of the
moon.

IF I WERE AN ANGEL

If I were an angel I'd sit by your side,

Controlling your thoughts and being your
guide,

I'd be your saviour I'd prove you're not
weak,

And the future you hold is not so bleak,

If you follow a pattern of positive thought,

Don't focus on battles that you have fought,

Draw strength from negative situations,

Use positive words and affirmations,

If I were an angel I'd take your pain,

I'd make you feel like living again,

I'd lift your spirit and find you peace,

And negative feelings would gently cease,

I'd teach you that life has twists and turns,

That everyone sometimes crashes and burns,

I'd teach u how to evolve again,

To focus on future and not your pain,

I'm not an angel, I'm a trusted friend

Who wants you to see that it's not the end,

It's time for you to spread your wings,

Focus on life's beautiful things,

The gift of life is precious to all,

So now it's time for you to stand tall,

Move forward now with hope in your heart,

And promise to make a a brand new start,

Learn to live, to love yourself,

And then you will find your ultimate wealth,

In loving yourself for who you are,

You'll rid of your demons and find your star

You'll glow in the dark and shine in the day,

The tears will stop I hope and pray,

Whenever you're feeling overwrought,

Refer to this poem, be

Less distraught

It will help you gain strength, move forward
with grace

To tackle the issues you have to face,

It will make you realise your weakness and
strength

It will make you analyse life at length

Your worthy of love and lots of friends

And this is where the story ends

So remember my friend shine through your
tears

Respect yourself and loose your
fears

For life will present you a
positive sign
Believe in your self and you will be fine!

Love.

Love yourself

As you should

Love your all

Love your good

Love your bad

Love your right

Love your peace

Love your fight

Love your devil

Love Your God

Love your normal

Love your odd

Love every piece

And every part

Love Mind and Soul

Body and Heart

Love the world

Even the sin

Love everything

Without and within

With no exception

And no denial

The true test

The true trial

I tell you Love

I tell you true

Is all we

Need ever woo

For the only way

To ever find you

Is to make love

All you do

Love Truth

Always

Thank you

Thank you for leading this journey,

And all the time we shared.

Thanks for the laughter and cries,

Not one emotion spared.

We may not know our destination,

But we enjoy being in God's creation.

We flit and fly, not letting a single moment
go by,

We savour every moment,

Always stopping to say "hi".

We will gladly watch a movie about you and
me,

But the ending we won't know
unfortunately.

Life can take us in different directions,

So hold me close and don't let go.

So don't forget this journey is a story with no script,

If acted correctly, the ending we can depict.

EPILOGUE: FREE SPIRIT

An independent person, who thinks for themselves. And rarely conform to society. They are quite optimistic lovers, who fight for what they believe. A fierce friend to have indeed. They're intuitive and comfortable in their own skin. And have a smile that shines from deep within.

Sweet Dreams Valentine.

Close your eyes, touch your heart. Make a wish, from the very start.
Let it be known, darling that you don't have to be whole, in order to shine. Kneel and pray and look up to the moon
And stars, for a soulful love so divine.

Everyone Needs a Hug.

A hug does so many things. It can bring joy and comfort, for those who get them. So here's a hug, a gift from me to you. A special reminder that I'm thinking of you.

As you are someone special to me. You'll never have to beg for anything. Not my time, not my attention, not my love. For everything I give to you willingly, because loving you is killing me.